what's sweeter

by june tate

KATHERINE TEGEN BOOKS
An Imprint of HarperCollins Publishers

what's sweeter

than the soft spot

behind a cat's ear

or a dog

who just wants to be close

what's sweeter

than a hammock

under a shady tree

or when a ladybug

lands on your arm

what's sweeter

than a fire truck

getting a bath

or seeing a bluebird

right outside

your window

what's sweeter than

finally getting something

you've been practicing

or how little ducks

walk in a row

what's sweeter

than a turtle

eating a salad

or when something

fits you just right

what could be sweeter

than the feeling you get

when you do something

you really like

and you forget

about everything else

or when you get a hug

from someone

you haven't seen

in a very long time

is there anything sweeter

than a letter from a friend

or a big bowl

of oranges

you picked yourself

or how

you never quite know

what color the sunset might be

at the end of the day

i can't imagine anything sweeter

no, nothing could be sweeter

except maybe you

To Pearl

Katherine Tegen Books is an imprint of HarperCollins Publishers.

What's Sweeter
Copyright © 2022 by June Tate
All rights reserved. Manufactured in Italy.
No part of this book may be used or reproduced in any manner
whatsoever without written permission except in the case of
brief quotations embodied in critical articles and reviews. For
information address HarperCollins Children's Books, a division of
HarperCollins Publishers, 195 Broadway, New York, NY 10007.
www.harpercollinschildrens.com

Library of Congress Control Number: 2021947079
ISBN 978-0-06-311413-5
The artist used pen, colored pencil, Copic marker, watercolor, and
Adobe Photoshop to create the digital illustrations for this book.

Typography by Chelsea C. Donaldson
22 23 24 25 26   RTLO   10 9 8 7 6 5 4 3 2 1
❖
First Edition